PETALS
of a
Rose

Inspirational Vignettes & Embellishments
For One Traveling in Search of Self

ATIYA

Atiya's Light Publishing
www.atiyaslight.com
info@atiyaslight.com

Library of Congress Control Number: 2014943838
ISBN: 978-0-9916444-4-5

Printed in the United States of America

For my fellow travelers on the path to enlightenment.

Acknowledgments

Expressions of appreciation and gratitude, for those who helped bring this book into fruition.

Table of Contents

Preface

I have never encountered a human being who was not searching for the deeper truths or meanings of life. Whether the quest was a private one or shared, the truth is every one of us has at some point thought about things that if verbalized might appear odd or offbeat. *Petals of a Rose* is a book that challenges you to think about the sometimes unthinkable or unspeakable and confront your own feelings or thoughts about a subject matter. It's a book that takes the sometimes odd or quirky things and inspires you to explore it honestly from a more profound and deeper perspective. By examining such topics as light versus dark, or exploring such popular questions as "which came first the chicken or the egg," *Petals of a Rose* gives way for you to go within your own self and discover your own extraordinary reverie.

This book actually unfolded over time. As I experienced life and had thoughts about a variety of things, I wrote them down. I was completely open, uninhibited, and forgiving with myself. I was completely free with the process. I even ventured back to a time when I was ten years of age allowing my thoughts to be what they were at that moment as I reflected. In the process I was able to confront the evolution of my own thoughts and how they could be one thing yesterday and something else today. It was an amazing journey because I was able to look in retrospect and solve some today mysteries. I also learned a greater level of acceptance of myself and others and the vast difference in how people think. I learned that it is truly okay to be me. What an enlightening and liberating experience. So I thought to myself, "This is something worth sharing with the world." So... here it is, *Petals of a Rose.*

As you read this book, I suggest that you not stop at what I am sharing. I implore you to go deeper within your own thoughts and discover yourself more fully in the process. Take on your own thoughts. Embrace them fully and completely! Perhaps you might end up writing your own book of embellishments! See, I happen to believe that you too are uncommonly beautiful and it is that uncommon part of yourself that the world is yearning to see. I know I am. Trust me when I say this, when you explore your own internal workings, you will most definitely discover an amazing and magical place that if nothing else will leave you purely entertained!

Enjoy the magic and the journey!

With Much Love,
Atiya

Author's Note

Every life experience is a wonderful opportunity to learn and grow. Our accomplishments and the endeavors we embark upon come out of either inspiration or disappointment. Nonetheless, all things work for good.

When others cross our path, they touch us in profound ways. The roles they play significantly helps to shape and mold us into the person we ultimately become. Strength, character, integrity, courage, spirit, humility, heart, and love allow us to learn those important lessons. Let the trials challenge you to become better. Let your achievements encourage you to celebrate the rewards of hard work. Be blessed to live better, do better, and love better. Be blessed to continue your journey sharing your best self with the world; and be ever so grateful for everyone you meet because they serve as vital instruments in the opus of your life.

Darkness Versus The Light

If I walk into a dark room I have never been in before, my reality for that room is darkness. It's possible to perceive more than darkness by relying on the senses of touch, sound, smell, taste, and to a degree – sight. Yet, to do so is only my perception, which is not always the reality or truth. I can accept the darkness; but it would limit my ability to learn more about the room and what's in it.

In truth, I do not know for sure what is actually in the dark room. However, I can imagine based on my ability to perceive things and situations, and based on past experiences. Nonetheless, it is still conjecture. If I conclude that darkness is all there is in that room, and there is no other possibility with respect to it, then my reality for the room will be darkness. Therefore, I will only experience darkness therein because I have ended any investigation, analysis, and consideration on the matter. Yet, the real truth of the room is still hidden.

Ascertaining the actual truth about the room and what is in it requires darkness to be dispelled. In order to eliminate darkness, the lights must be turned on. Once the lights are on, one can more readily "see" what is present in the room. Yet, that is dependent upon their faculty of sight being intact and whether or not their experiences in life have afforded them the knowledge to be able to identify various objects and effectively make distinctions between them. It also depends on their ability to reason and measure things accurately and their capacity to perceive things in the proper perspective. Perhaps they may be able to more precisely discern the color of the walls; whether the floors are hardwood, carpeted or tiled; what type of room it is (kitchen, bathroom, bedroom, den, warehouse, etc.).

While the senses may give an indication of the type of room or what is contained within it, the truth can only be verified by the presence of light being shined and then by one's ability to discriminate. Once the lights have been turned on, apparent darkness is no longer the reality. However, unless one is able to comprehend what is visually obvious in the room, darkness still exists.

For a visually impaired or blind person, it doesn't matter whether the light switch is flipped on or off, with the physical eye, perhaps with the exceptions of a few fractions of light, they still normally experience a dark room. A blind person has not the faculty of visual perception, and thus, must use other methods to determine the truth of the room. A profoundly deaf person is unable to hear through "normal" channels, the music that may be melodically playing. A person who has not the sense of touch, smell or taste, is likewise in need of accommodation to ascertain the bona-fide and authentic truth of the room and experience the new reality of the lights being turned on.

Questions:

1. If a person is deaf, dumb and blind, what is necessary to help their reality of darkness, be transformed by the light?

2. If a blind man has never experienced light and has never distinguished light from darkness, what methods do you use to help him comprehend and discriminate between the two realities– light and darkness?

3. If a blind man is seeking the light, but unable to see it no matter what accommodations are made, who do you fault, the blind man who only knows darkness or the seeing man who is bringing the light?

4. Who is more at fault - a blind man who is seeking truth but can't find it; a man who can see but refuses to accept truth; or a man who sees and comprehends both darkness and light, but refuses to give truth and light?

Yin and Yang's Inner Sanctity

As we search the depths and essence of our beings, it is impossible to deny the splendor and beauty that lies deep within. While man in his divine state is the ruler and powerful force that calls to attention and into submission everything in his sight, reach, and touch, it's equally phenomenal to behold the female in her transcendent state.

Her prowess is beyond reproach, as she masters how to execute and deliver through a world of subtleties that which she intends. She holds the power of arousal and deliberately baits whom she seeks, yet skillfully guides to the upper room of spiritual enlightenment. While her physical beauty is one to bathe in, her magnetic appeal is directly linked to her connection with the Creator.

Her shyness exists simply because the mining or extracting process has yet to be completed. While the vices appear to weaken the divinity of the female, they are in truth a cover waiting to be removed and darkness pleading for light. The introvert, like Lazarus and the sleeping giant, is simply waiting on the call from the Savior to "RISE!" She too, must be quickened by the breath of life. She too, must be set free.

Resolution is the answer. To resolve the vices that cover her divinity means exposing, facing, and overcoming all that hinders her rise. Purpose is the pathway to setting the introverted female free. A woman who has overcome hard times, sexism, exploitation, rape, molestation, lies, abuse, depression, oppression, slander, loneliness, drugs, alcohol, and the like, has in truth already transformed by the renewing of her mind. She has reached an elevated state of existence, and is climbing higher still.

In her divine state, woman is the womb of man. She is an environment made ready and prepared for God - man in his exalted state. She is like triple darkness, where The One creates over and over again. Like air or a gentle-yet forceful breeze, she is inspired to continue to bring forth life like springtide.

The beauty of it all is that wherever she is, he is too. Wherever there is woman, there is man. The best and most divine of it all is that wherever there is harmony between the two, there is also the presence of The One.

Character and Manners

A person may be attentive to changing clothes on a daily basis as a matter of "good" hygiene; but how does that relate to the caliber of person you are? One's character is a mark that is worn consistently regardless of the day of the week. To change character regularly as a matter of practice would demonstrate inconsistency and cause another not to trust you.

There is a code of conduct that every individual operates within. Personally I choose to function from the power that lies within. What about you? What are your prevailing customs and habits? A Code of Conduct is "a set of rules outlining the responsibilities of or proper practices for an individual." Doctors take the Hippocratic Oath; Buddhists adhere to the five, eight or ten Precepts; writers follow the Journalist's Creed. There is even a biblical principle or "Ethic of Reciprocity," often referred to as the "Golden Rule." Although, some may argue that this rule doesn't adequately shape one's behavior toward good manners. Their justification for that position is based on the fact of what the Golden Rule states: "Do unto others as you would have them do unto you." It encourages a person to give in return what was given.

I presume this may be very effective in cases where people are only engaging in "good" manners; but what about when someone is inordinately rude or intolerable? There is a book of spiritual wisdom which states "When a (courteous) greeting is offered you, meet it with a greeting still more courteous, or (at least) of equal courtesy. God takes careful account of all things." Many have pondered over that question. For this reason, it may be that some men of valor embraced and championed the "Silver Rule," which states - Do No Harm!

Minding your manners and good character goes beyond the principle of reciprocity. It is a superior way of being that resolves one to behave honorably regardless of the actions of others. There is a clear distinction between those with manners and those without them. This ultimately is the principle that all divine texts encourage.

"Those who quit their proper character to assume what does not belong to them are, for the greater part, ignorant both of the character they leave and of the character they assume." (Bovee, n.d.).

Therefore, let not your good character be like the clothes you wear and something you take on or off. Sages, saviors, masters, and prophets come that we may experience a more abundant life. They bring truths that can change lives for the better and bring humanity into a higher level of awareness and consciousness. However, a person's condition only changes, when they themselves alter it.

To change your reality, it's necessary to manifest something different than what you are currently disclosing. To mind your manners is to pay attention to how you conduct yourself. There are many ways in which a person may behave. There are countless styles that one could employ when responding to certain situations. Yet, offering your personal best in each circumstance is a gift that far outweighs exacting outward tradition. The formalities of "appropriate" behavior, is a definitive art. Nonetheless, to develop a keen sense of awareness of one's self and their impact on the world is an ability that everyone must master.

The spirit of excellence is not merely measured by how proficiently one sets a table or precisely lays their napkin across their lap. The heart of fineness and brilliance, quality and distinction, is determine by one's character and manner of being - which transcends basic convention. "Our characters are a result of our conduct." (Aristotle, c. 335 B.C.).

How we handle ourselves is a matter of record that is not easily expunged. Thus, the old English adage by Thomas Paine often rings true – "Character is easier kept than recovered." A person's character is the bona-fide truth and authentic reality of who they are. Your reputation is established from the opinions of others and like a shadow casts itself in your sphere wherever there is no light. Character lives in you. It is the substance of who you are; but your shadow is what stands behind you whenever you conceal your light.

The Primordial Triangle

One day three forces got together and came up with an idea. The older force decided that it would serve as counselor and guide to the other two. The younger two forces accepted the challenge to do the most strenuous part of the work to bring the idea alive. All three agreed that no one was more important than the other. They knew and understood very clearly that it would take the three of them working together for any of them to be successful. They accepted the realities of one another and agreed to each stay in their own lane as they began the arduous journey of making their shared vision a reality.

The three forces, all in consort, immediately went to work and started on their way.

The two younger forces at this point began their tedious struggle to conceptualize the details of this idea. The third force was very much present ensuring that the right energy was put into the creation of a very clear, concise and accurate picture of what the three agreed upon. After a lot of hard work and constant nurturing of their idea over time, they came together and determined that it was time to involve you in the process. So the three forces had a very important meeting, which was paramount in shaping what you would look like, how you would be and when you would come about. At the conclusion of that meeting, the three forces knew without a shadow of a doubt that they had just laid the foundation of a whole new reality and that their most magnificent idea was bound to change the world!

You are an idea conceived in truth and manifested in real time. What started as a thought in someone else's mind became YOU - an amazing reality and fruit of thought empowered with the same ability to conceptualize, create and manifest. About every 300 milliseconds, a thought enters the human mind. Brilliant ideas flash on an almost constant basis, yet a small fraction is acted upon by even the greatest among us. Can you imagine if every intuitive idea that came across your mind was carried into fruition and manifested? Your ideas are the pathway to your destiny. If you follow through with even just half of them, your life will sky-rocket into another whole dimension.

You will begin to lead an extraordinary life because you made that very important decision to A.C.T. – Accept the Challenge to Thrive. Those three forces worked collectively and cooperatively together, synergistically and harmoniously to empower you to come forth. Yet, while you were just a concept, you still took shape and that is because you were a determined thought.

Life is wonderful and full of amazing adventures and opportunities. You can live your dream and reach optimal potential. You were born to make a major impact in the world. Yet it starts with bringing your true and whole self to the table, meaning your three-dimensional self – Body, Mind, and Spirit. Like the three forces, all three must be in harmony and cooperation.

BODY – The Human Dimension You
(The Manifested Reality)

In order for anything else in your life to be of any substance, you must have a clear understanding of who YOU are and your connection to this wonderful universe. Some people believe that it is others outside of themselves that determines their value. However, it is how well you manifest the excellence and light that is within you that determines your worth at that moment. Every human being was created with greatness and has potential for greatness beyond measure. We were all born with a specific gift to enhance the world in a dynamic way. Now is the time to unleash the vast greatness that is within you. Decide the physical manifestation or projection of internal light that you choose to walk in.

MIND – The Imaginative and Creative You
(The Working Reality)

Mind is the seat of your thoughts, perceptions, memories, emotions, will and imagination. It is your stream of consciousness. A sound mind is essential to overall personal wholeness. The first step to having a sound mind is proper nourishment. If your mind's sole sustenance consist of negativity, doubt and idleness, then what comes from you will be very much the same. A sound mind is one that is positive, fit and feeding on those things which inspires, motivates, uplifts and produces a desire for creativity.

A healthy state of mind allows you to thoroughly filter and process information, as well as make clearer and more concise decisions and judgments. In a positive mind environment, the lasting impressions that are stored are more productive and constructive. Determine what you are feeding your mind and think about who is preparing the meals.

Healthy mind food includes:

*Constructive conversations and dialogue
*Loyalty and honesty
*Mindfulness
*Optimism
*Organization
*Positivity and a positive attitude

*Spirituality

Unhealthy mind food includes:

*Gossip and slack-talk
*Backbiting and slander
*Negativity
*Poor attitude
*Pessimism
*Worldliness
*Clutter

In addition to the proper feeding of your mind, it is also important to exercise it on a daily basis. By working out your mind, you provide it with favorable stimulation that awakens you to life and all of its extraordinary experiences. The more "fit" your mind is, the more you come alive and become more energetic, hopeful, and cheerful in your spirit. What are some of the things that you do to stimulate your mind in a positive way?

Other ways you can exercise your mind includes:

*Cultivating your gifts, talents and skills

*Learning; the stimulation of intellectual properties

*Problem solving and resolving conflicts

*Being creative

*Playing strategic games such as scrabble, taboo, word
  and crossword puzzles

*Applying your mind to the development of your
  body and spirit

You may be able to list many more ways to exercise
your mind. That's great! However, a mind all worked-out
and not relaxed is a mind that is all stressed-out. Therefore, it is equally necessary to relax your mind; and that
frankly, is the part that so many have struggled with at one
time or another. Can you imagine lifting weights, running,
walking on the treadmill or bicycling for 8-16 hours a day
straight? Well, that is exactly what we do when we engage
our minds during the course of a day and not take a "time
out" to relax.

Relaxation provides that cool down we need to un-
wind, releasing the pressure from the stress that naturally
comes from exercising our minds. It rejuvenates us to get
back to it with consistency and vigor, which ultimately

helps us to move forward with vivacity. If that's all you do is work, work, work and take no time to relax, it will most certainly show in your disposition, as well as the results, outcome and quality of your work, not to mention your health.

Do yourself and others around you a favor. Relax! You deserve it. It is one of the daily rewards that you give to yourself for working so hard. You might find that you will like yourself more and others will too.

Some ways to relax your mind includes:

*Taking a coffee, tea or lunch break

*Meditating

*Taking a nap

*Watching something "light" on television

*Playing (non-analytical) games

*Going for a stroll

*Taking deep breaths

*Cuddling

*Having sex (If you're married of course)

*Taking a bubble bath

*Getting a massage

*Taking a train or boat ride

*Enjoying a rocker, swing or hammock

*Doing crafts, hobbies, or little passions

*Watching a fish tank

*Taking a walk on the beach

Your mind is too remarkable to waste by not using it or misusing it. When we give our minds the proper nourishment, exercise and relaxation, we will find that we think more clearly, our perceptions are keener and more accurate, our memory is sharper, our emotions more under control, our will stronger, and our imagination more vivid. Now, how about that for a balanced mind?

SPIRIT – The In-Purpose You
(The Ultimate Reality)

Your spirit is the "God Messenger" within you. It's that supernatural aspect of yourself that helps you to achieve what appears to be impossible. Your spirit is your knowing self; that guiding force that is cognizant, aware, and operates only in truth.

Portals of Enlightenment

This is a journey to spiritual awakening, healing and overall well-being. So, my friend and fellow traveler, I want to bestow upon you information to help as you continue on the path to enlightenment. There is so much to share, yet I will keep it simple.

We are spiritual beings experiencing a material world. There are many dimensions in this universe and what a lovely experience it is to vibrate on a plane of existence that brings you the abundance and universal love of the Creator. The Ultimate Law of the Universe is Love. It's all around us if we would just open our eyes - third eye that is and receive the beautiful blessings. For the one working to lose weight, it's so much more than shedding physical pounds. It is a journey like no other and if you are mindful through the process, it truly is one that allows you to see more clearly.

The third eye is also referred to as the "inner eye" or "eye of the heart." This eye allows you to see divine light and truth. Prayer and meditation are constant channels for communion with The One; and no matter what position you're in or direction you face, it is full surrender that allows your whole being to walk in the light. The portal or "gate" of entry is the five senses. This information is like small fractions of light to help you open up in order to access the entry way leading to your higher self. This is a realm where you can fly.

I am an oracle who has been sent to help you recognize the portals. Like you, no one really truly knows who I am except The One who sent me. However, I am making myself known as I remember more and more each day. Why don't you? It must be understood that it's much more to walking in the light than touching, seeing, hearing, smelling and tasting. The portals are designed to enhance your intuitiveness, insight, and perception. Pay attention to see the miracles in the process. Yes, pay attention as you travel in the material realm. Also be mindful as you travel in the light. Remember to be present and in the moment.

There is so much to share. However, perhaps another time we will get the chance. For now, imbibe in this moment. Now, let's get to the information. Consider these little gifts that open up your five senses: Hearing, Sight, Smell, Taste, and Touch. I will talk about them in reverse order.

Portal of Touch: The Gift of the Healing Stones & Power of Protection

The portal of touch is the protective barrier between internal and external. Here I give you two very important healing stones for your journey: Citrine and Green Aventurine. The Citrine Healing Stone has wonderful metaphysical properties that help you to align with your higher self and changes negative energy into positive energy. You will find that your power of intuition is greatly enhanced.

Citrine encourages happiness, hope and laughter; stabilizes emotion; calms anger and frustration; removes fears; helps with overcoming nightmares; and encourages a good night sleep. It is referred to as the "Merchant Stone," and is very powerful in attracting prosperity and success. Citrine also has physical properties that you may want to explore should you be inspired to experience the gift of touching one.

The Green Aventurine Healing Stone is an electrifying experience as well. It benefits all areas of creativity, imagination, intellect and mental clarity. It also helps one to see alternatives in trying situations giving a positive outlook, courage and inner strength. This stone is an enhancer and brings career success and friendship to one's life. This is a gentle stone that gives a sense of calm, balance and happiness. It has protection energies. It too has tremendous physical properties. Again, you can explore those should you want to touch one.

Portal of Taste: The Gift of Chocolate Cake & Power of Discernment

The portal of taste is the tool for discerning subtleties. Here I offer you a piece of chocolate cake. You choose the slice that is best for you. Enjoy it to the very last bite. Chocolate is sweet, heavenly and adventurous. Give yourself the pleasure of simple delights without the addiction. Taste the integral parts of this magnificent dessert, each balancing out the other. Imagine having chocolate anytime you wanted it without putting on a single pound. That is what this journey helps you to do.

Like other things in life, chocolate cake is a comfort food craved by many to soothe an aching soul. It's not really an addiction to chocolate that some suffer from; it is rather a yearning for something missing to which chocolate happily fills the void. To come to an understanding of your soul song, restore the balance in your being and give your soul what's missing. When this happens, you will not crave chocolate; you will choose it as a matter of choice, and experience the pleasure of it freely and within reason.

Portal of Smell: The Gift of Organic Healing Soap & Power of Intuition

The portal of smell strengthens intuition and perception. This lavender bar of healing soap is to positively influence your mental, emotional, physical, and metaphysical state. It will bring clarity, peace of mind, and emotional balance. There are also physical properties for men, women, and children. The lavender essential oil brings out the best healing properties in other essential oils it is blended with. So feel free to explore the refreshing aromas of other soaps which contain essential oils.

Portal of Sight: The Gift of Color & Power of Transformation

The portal of sight brings understanding and allows you to experience the beauty of divine light. It bridges the gap between the physical and transcendent realms. Manifest your inner creator through the wavelengths of light. Color impacts our mood and has an effect on everything around us.

Pilot in purple. Uplift yourself and others. Calm the mind and nerves. Gain a sense of direction and be creative.

Run in red. Be enthusiastic. Be energetic. Take action and stand with confidence. You are protected from your fears. Be not anxious.

Balance in black. Know that you have potential and that all things are possible. It's a mystery that allows you to be inconspicuous when you need to be and provides you with a restful emptiness.

Awaken in White. Become mentally alert and clear. No more clutter or obstacles. Evoke your power to purifying thoughts and actions. Enjoy the fresh beginnings.

Quietly Comfort in Aqua. Offer yourself and others peace through the calming and soothing rhythm of youth, fidelity, hope and health. Dance in the strength of idealism, confidence, and clarity of mind. Speak clearly and communicate truthfully. Explore the endless possibilities of life and love by learning to pain with the colors of the wind.

Portal of Hearing: The Gift of Awakening & Power of Prayer and Meditation

The portal of hearing enhances the power of prayer and meditation. It also tunes up your spiritual insight and strengthens discernment. Your portals have been opened. Now free your mind, clear your mind and heart to receive a very beautiful message. The next audio that peeks your interest or the next sound of music that you are guided to, get it. Remove the perception of the person who is delivering the message and everything you know about them. Simply embrace the principle of the work of art and how it applies to your life at this moment. Let the experience help you move beyond the physical vessel and all of his/her imperfections and embrace light as a child of light. Learn to move by the spirit.

Remembering the Inner Child

While visiting a school on my journey, I came across the path of a little girl about five years of age. On my way out, I decided to take the opportunity to go to the "little girls' room." This is naturally where I saw a beautiful and peculiar little person. As I began to wash my hands, I noticed that she was standing on a chair wiping her mouth and looking into the mirror, paying very close attention to the details of the spot of dirt she was so carefully removing from around her mouth.

One of the teachers came in and noticed the little girl and asked, "Why are you standing on the chair like that?" The little girl with surety replied, "Because I like looking at myself in the mirror." The teacher turned to look at me, her eyes widened and then she simply shrugged her shoulders and left the room. Tickled at the young girl's response, I slowly dried my hands and continued to carefully observe her staring at herself in the mirror. After a moment, I asked the little girl, "What are you looking at?" She replied, "Me." Then I asked her, "Who is me?" She responded with much confidence, "You." I smiled and asked what she meant.

The little girl looked up for a moment as if thinking on what I had asked her. Finally, I asked her, "Are you saying that you are me and I am you?" With firm resolution, she responded, "Yes!" We gave each other a high five and I told her that I loved her, then, walked out of the room leaving her standing in the mirror to continue her quest.

As I reflected later on the experience of just watching the little girl, I realized that the words of this beautiful little butterfly were simple, yet very profound. While she may not have fully understood the magnitude of what she had just spoken, she was going about her day as little girls often do. She was open, completely transparent with a certain naivety, and innocence - the way all children are when they are free to grow.

There is an unseen power of mercy and love that somehow reaches out to touch us in the most magnificent and creative ways. As women, we are all God's little girls. As men, you are all vicegerents being primed to rule a kingdom created especially for you. It is the same openness, transparency, and truthfulness that this child demonstrated, that we must discover as adults. Some of us have certainly forgotten about the child within. So many people lose that innocence due to the harshness of the world. Yet, in order to discover or rediscover the beauty that has been placed within, you must look into the proverbial mirror; remove every spot of dirt you see, and cultivate the wonderful and divine gifts that was bestowed upon you.

Lessons are learned at any age, and truth transcends time. The butterfly begins life as an earthly creature, then, becomes obscured from view in the chrysalis while the power of unseen hands works diligently to transform this seemingly insignificant creature into a lovely work of art. Just as a caterpillar must die before it can emerge as a brilliant butterfly, we too must leave old ways behind that we may become new creatures in The One.

A butterfly represents the timeless beauty of a woman, and the supreme power of her fascination lies in the sweetness and grace of her refinement. Being a woman is a most spectacular experience. At any age, she is an embodiment of virtue and a priceless treasure. Her irresistible charm comes from her unyielding surrender to the Creator, and her willingness to be a vessel of abounding light. Age does not wither the fascinating woman, because a fascinating woman is consistent in her walk. Her light is a manifestation of the Divine light burning gloriously within her. She illuminates the spirit of The One in her very being. Like the metamorphosis of the butterfly, she mystically transforms into a lovely work of art and walks confidently in the power of her divine nature being...Fascinating!

The process of this astounding transformation from caterpillar to butterfly represents the creative power and dominion of the man. His strength and power lies in the integrity and honor of his scepter. Being a man is a most humbling experience. Through the latitude of his experience is born courage and vigor. His stature and respect comes from the complete alignment with the Creator, and his willingness to walk consistently in the light. Time does not deflate him, because he grows in wisdom as each day passes. He becomes he who lives within. Like the metamorphosis of the butterfly, he mystically rules his kingdom and walks confidently with the authority of his divine nature being…Supreme!

The butterfly and the process of transformation can easily be witnessed in the children's garden where all the tiny caterpillars are diligently spinning their wondrous and stupendous time machines. Therein they innocently leave the lessons of time. In life's little garden of treasures for all to discover is the miracle of learning the lesson of remembering the inner child.

The Lesson of the Butterfly

Note to the reader:

The lesson of the butterfly is an adaptation of a story whose author is unknown.

One day a little girl came across a chrysalis. She noticed as she looked upon this house of wonder, a beautiful butterfly struggling to free itself. As she watched in awe, she could no longer stand by as this tiny, yet fragile creature toiled. Thus, seeing the butterfly labor with such persistence and determination, the little girl decided to help by minimizing its efforts. She then made an incision in the chrysalis just large enough for the butterfly to break free, rescuing it from the obvious pain and exertion of coming forth.

At last, this fragile life germ was free! The little girl was so proud of her good deed that she ran home to show her mother the butterfly. She burst into the front door yelling, "Ummu, Mudarrissa!"

Her mother came out to see what the commotion was all about.

"Yes Nashida," she said, noticing the child's excitement.

"I set a butterfly free, I set a butterfly free!"

Her mother examined the butterfly very carefully. She noticed that its wings were withered, and this poor living thing was unable to fly. The little girl in her enthusiasm had not observed the condition of the butterfly. Watching her mother intently, she followed her to the front porch, sat on the step in bewilderment and wondered what she had done.

The little girl's mother, responding to her child's expression, pulled her close, and sat the butterfly gently on a leaf.

"Nashida," she said. "Do you see this beautifully-colored creature?"

"Yes, Mudarrissa." The child responded in hopeful anticipation.

"Well," said the mother. "This butterfly is a very special creature, indeed. Yet it is not born a butterfly. Initially, it starts out as a caterpillar, and through a most fascinating process, over time, in obscurity and hidden from view, the caterpillar transforms into a beautiful work of art – we call butterfly. This exquisite living thing, as it flies, has extraordinary power and strength. It even has an intuitive nature to sense an impending storm."

"Wow!" said the young girl. "But Mudarrissa, why won't this butterfly fly?"

"You see, Nashida, as a butterfly pushes itself through the tiny opening of the chrysalis, fluid is pushed from its distended body to its wings, making it possible to fly."

"Tell me more, Ummu, Mudarrissa." The little girl said with a great deal of eagerness.

"If this process of struggle does not happen, the fluid becomes trapped in the body, making it too heavy; and the wings would be deprived of fluid necessary for strength and balance to be able to support and lift the weight of the body." The mother continued. "And although this little butterfly that you have befriended appeared to be working very hard to break free, it takes a tremendous amount of effort to fly. This struggle prepares the butterfly for its journey in life, and my child, so it is with us."

This is the end of the story, but not of the message. We too are like this amazing lesson of nature from the butterfly. Our beginnings may seem small and appear insignificant, yet as we surrender to The One, and submit ourselves to a transformation process, we become new. However, without the unyielding exertion to overcome difficulty and struggles in life, we remain paralyzed, not being able to experience the joy of flight.

Struggle is something that happens in life. While our desire may be ease, it is through our toiling that we achieve excellence. Struggle produces the spirit of humility, and humility is the launching pad for success. The greatest rewards come after we have worked very hard, and exerted great effort to achieve our goals.

A mother witnesses the gift of life after she labors to bring forth her child. The farmer enjoys a plenteous harvest after he diligently tills his land. And yes, the butterfly enjoys the sweet, sweet nectar as it flies from plant to plant carrying pollen, after it frees itself from the chrysalis. As human beings, our struggles are obstacles that strengthen us and help us to prepare for our purpose in life. Transformation takes place through the process of overcoming difficulty. This is why it's important to stay the course. Your desire to reach the goal must be greater than the struggle it will take to get there.

Like the caterpillar that turns into a beautiful butterfly, we too undergo a complete change in form, structure, and function as we go through our own re-birth process. This takes much effort. In order to take flight, and grow into our greatness, we must be willing to face and overcome difficulty. Like the butterfly, our brilliance, which is cultivated out of the vicissitudes of life, becomes a magnificent reflection and expression of a higher power. This lesson of the butterfly is one that can be learned in a special place where only a child's heart can go. In the children's garden, where all the little lovelies play, miracles take place and escapes the obvious intrusions of those not well intended.

Unseen hands devise a class without walls, without desks, pens or paper. The tool is simply one's imagination and three invisible classrooms of learning: Orientation,

Stabilization, and Realization. Orientation is the introduction to a new reality and idea. Stabilization is the process of helping the new student of imagination's class become fixed, adapted, and adjusted to that new idea. This supports a continuous inclination to the new way of life they are learning and enables them to remain steadfast on their journey. Realization is the bringing forth from the womb of the mind the phenomenal creations of masterful artistry originating in the repository where all miracles begin.

During conception, an egg is fertilized and must find its way to the uterus. The newly fertilized egg must find this resting place and be nurtured, kept safe and warm so that it can grow and come to term. Like a baby in the womb during the first trimester, the kindergartner in the children's garden must be carefully guarded that imagination can run supreme. They must be kept safe and warm. The seed of a new idea must be placed in the right environment, watered, provided sunlight, given love and nurtured. A great amount of care and concern is necessary during the process. What greater place for the Divine to plant than in the mind of a child both big and small a dream just waiting to be born!

Winning Isn't Everything

What's the one thing you think about when you are playing a game? Go ahead and say it! W-I-N-N-I-N-G. Most people who play a game or sports think most about winning. It's natural; but is that really what it's all about?

I remember at Roosevelt Junior High School, I played softball and basketball. I was also a cheerleader, but that doesn't count. I never did get the nerve to do a back flip without the trampoline, and well the splits, that's out of the question too. Anyway, with softball, I played short-stop and second base. During softball season, we practiced almost every day after school and had games every Saturday morning. Our team had to be at whatever baseball diamond the game was being played by 8:00 a.m. Whether it was an away game or a home game, we had to make our way there on our own. Most of the team members walked. Depending on where we lived, it could be between one to three miles. However, we always turned up ready to play. Some of us walked together. As we passed a team member's home we stopped and they joined in on the walk. We had a great team and we demonstrated our greatness by our winning streak. I think we ended up taking second place overall that season.

In basketball, I played point-guard. I started every game except our first tournament game. Interestingly enough, I had the same coach for basketball as I did for softball. Mr. Westendorf was an awesome coach. The team liked working with him; and I really liked working with him too. However, he made me pretty upset during one of the games. We just didn't see eye-to-eye.

Our basketball team went into the first tournament game at Trewyn School undefeated. Mr. Westendorf decided not to start me. My knickers didn't touch my backside. Talk about an attitude, mine was off the chain. The game was really intense. It was very challenging for me to sit on the bench. I had to swallow the fact that we were losing. There was this point guard on the other team that was quick. To me she was a hotshot, but she was making baskets in my team members' faces. We were falling further and further behind.

I begged coach to put me in. He ignored me and kept putting other players in the game. When he finally did put me in the game, it was the third quarter and we were about twenty points down. I was fast myself. Yet, I have to admit, that girl kept me on my toes. I was very competitive and determined for our team to win. I believed we could win. The ball was thrown inbound to me, we worked well as a team, but we had to play hard and smart in order to score points. While I was in the game, our team was coming back from behind. We were on a roll making basket-after-basket. Then all of a sudden, the whistle blew and here comes Carol taking my place in the game. Once again, I was anxiously sitting the bench.

I sat the bench until the last few minutes of the game. No amount of begging and pleading to get back in worked. Mr. Westendorf held his ground. Finally, in the last couple of minutes of the game, he let me play. We were down about ten points. We lost that game and naturally, I blamed Mr. Westendorf because if he had started me, we would have won. Of course, that was the rationale of a 13-year old.

Many years have gone by since Roosevelt. The time had come for me to go to basketball and volleyball games to watch my own children play. As a spectator, winning was still one of the most important things. When I went to my children's basketball games, I was the biggest cheerleader in the stands. Sometimes I wondered if they would throw me out of the gymnasium. When they announced the starting line-up, you should hear us. We were a group of parents that had camaraderie and our children could look up and see us right there in front or way at the top in the bleachers screaming "Go, Metcalf Wildcats!"

The mindset for winning was no different for my children's basketball team either. My son's basketball team was a very different situation because his team members were all hearing impaired. Attending his games offered a profound experience that transcended winning. As I watched my son playing basketball, we could hear the whistle blowing. It was a very puzzling thing because we knew that the players on our team could not hear. Yet, they were responding as if they could. Well into the game, I realized that the whistle was actually for the other team.

Our team was playing hearing peers and the whistle was for them. Our boys were being signaled by lights and colored flags.

As the team went to the sidelines, the cheerleaders graced the court. It didn't matter that they too were deaf. They happily supported the KSD Jack Rabbits. They cheered to the roaring beat of a drum. Everyone could feel the vibrations while the cheerleaders stepped in rhythm to the beat. Finally, Mr. Holland's Opus made sense.

It feels good to win, no doubt about it. However, there are many more incredible lessons one can gain from participating in sports and other competitive games. It's about empowerment, perseverance, character building, and fulfilling dreams. It's about inclusion, understanding, and compassion.

Mr. Westendorf taught the importance of being dependable, responsible and accountable. When you don't show up for practice you let your team down. The same is true for not being there when someone needs you. He taught the significance of team work, having good sportsmanship, and that there are more important lessons to be learned than winning. For winning is not always about the technicality of sports, but about demonstrating a winning character and the rewards of hard work, teamwork, dedication, and the importance of not giving up.

Seeing children play sports and witnessing how their eyes light up when they see you in the stands taught the importance of moral support, having someone who believes in you and willing to give their time as verification and demonstration of that belief. It taught the importance of consistency and trust. For a child, just knowing that your parents are going to be there for you, no matter how embarrassing they might be, is a feeling that goes a long way and one remembered for years to come. Seeing them present to cheer you on and being supportive whether you win or lose the game is priceless.

People who play sports come from diverse backgrounds and various walks of life. No matter what language they speak or what their country of origin is, participation in sports is a universal activity. Together it is something that the world celebrates! Whether playing, watching, or volunteering, sports empowers people in such a way that years from now they can look back not on whether or not their team won, but they might be able to stand and talk about the magical journey that sports took them on.

TO WIN, YES! It's an amazing feeling; but the magic in the process and how sports truly impacts a person's life can only be understood by getting involved! By virtue of getting involved in something so spectacular, makes you a winner!

People

Getting along with others who do not agree with you or share the same interests is something to ponder. It's much easier to connect with those who have similar interests and are not afraid to be themselves and allow you to be yourself. You can more readily make a connection when there is a common interest or like mind. Many people are able to form close relationships with others whom they can express themselves openly. Wonderful bonds are established in these cases and one can discover an unspeakable joy that is often nurtured over time.

What happens when you do not necessarily have any-thing in common? What goes through your mind when you are placed in a situation where you almost have to allocate some of your space and time to accommodate someone whom you really do not want to be around? Something to think about isn't it?

Personally speaking, I naturally and effortlessly tend to connect with people who are non-traditional and who others deem "odd, weird, or unusual." I find myself attracted to people who are very spiritual and freely express their spirituality no matter how "offbeat" it may appear to be to someone else. I build relationships where there is a mutual feeling of appreciation and safety, and where there is freedom of expression in a non-threatening environment. I find myself able to relate better and open up more with others when I am not confronted with the fear of judgment, feelings of having to "hide" the truth of how I feel for emotional safety's sake.

People who are quick to label another "crazy" or as one bringing drama is a connection to which I immediate-ly run the other direction. I'd rather be in the presence of someone who is secure in who they are and can appreciate me for who I am. Spending time with people who aren't looking for my faults all the time or constantly criticizing other people while in my company is probably the idea environment. This is not to say that I don't appreciate when people are able to express what is on their mind, whether it be positive or negative. That's not something to judge. Likewise, I have no problem with someone pointing out a personal shortcoming of mine, although I most likely saw it first. What I have an issue with is gossip and people who seem to dwell in the negative.

When people are able to be completely honest about their feelings and are strong enough to handle someone else being completely honest about theirs with them, whether they are in agreement or not, speaks volumes. These types of people help others grow because they are not afraid to point out the areas where improvements are needed. But keep in mind; some people don't want to spend all of their time hearing about what's wrong with them.

When there's no trust, personally I'd much rather not be in that person's company for any length of time because I wouldn't feel safe. I am not only talking about physical safety. I'm also referring to emotional and spiritual security as well. It's okay to develop strong bonds and friendships with people who don't agree with everything you stand for or who may not see the world exactly the way you do. It's a great experience to genuinely appreciate a person who is able to present another way of looking at things and are able to be who they are whether they agree with you or not. There is a very real and clear difference between disagreeing and being disagreeable. Disagreeable people are not fun to be around.

I prefer to spend time with people who are of like minds. When I say like minds, I don't mean they have to be like me. I am saying I'd rather be around people who have similar lifestyles and share some of the same interests. I seek to build principled relationships that transcend all sorts of labels. Yet, I do prefer and seek out relationships with people who have somewhat of the same family structure as I do. As a married woman, I desire friendships with married couples that my husband and I can bond with and develop a healthy friendship with. It is important to me for those married couples to be in healthy marriages because this is one of my greatest desires. Having a strong, healthy, happy, joyous marriage and family is fundamentally important to me. While I may have single friends, I do not seek them out and I place very clear boundaries in those friendships.

This brings me to another point to ponder about people. Have you considered who you keep company with daily? Some people are always surrounded by a whole lot of people. They wouldn't feel whole or fulfilled if there was not always someone around them. For me, I rather keep my circle very small. Feeling safe and secure emotionally and otherwise is critical in my world. I much rather have my daily circle filled with my immediate family. Now, this does not negate my desire for friendships, or the pleasure I enjoy when keeping company with them, it just means I prefer to keep my "inner" circle or "nucleus" my family. Amazingly, there have been a few very close friends who have been like family; they too have been a part of my inner circle.

I like to make friends, yet I am cautious. I also enjoy entertaining business colleagues, associates, and others; however I am not interested in keeping company with them on a consistent daily basis, no more than they are interested in keeping company with me on a daily basis. Some people refer to their job and where they work as their second home. They also consider their co-workers their other family or their friends. This is not the case for me. Work is work and home is home. There are clear boundaries and I make a real distinction between the two.

Some people feel it's overwhelming to nurture a lot of close relationships at one time because of the amount of energy they tend to give in relationships. This does not mean that they don't enjoy the company of others. For them it's a matter of overload. Then there are some who have favorite people they like to spend time with or best friends, while many others take their spouse as their best friend. Personally, my friendships tend to have longevity. People who are close to me have usually been there for ten to twenty years.

A third thing to ponder is the important role both young and the old play in your life. I thought about this. As you study people, you can see a variety of attributes which can put you in awe. When people operate within their purpose and are utilizing their divine gifts for the benefit of themselves, their family, and the world, it's truly a miracle.

Older people represent wisdom and guidance. They have something extra that only comes with age. It is possible for older people to be foolish, but I don't recall ever meeting any. People who have lived for many years have a lot to share, and I like to hear it. I have met several women over 100-years of age. I loved it! They seemed to love me too. I could sit and talk with them for a while. They were in their right mind too. Now that is how I want to be when I reach that age.

Young people also amuse me. They keep me looking at things from a fresh and new perspective. When I study children, I learn and understand so much by simply observing. They have such creative imaginations in their play. Anything is possible in their world. The heart of a child is one to keep no matter how old you are. People who have lived over a hundred tend to have this type of carriage. The young can help you believe in the "make believe" and the impossible. The old can take you to the world of make believe and show you that all things are possible when you believe.

The most challenging of people to deal with are teenagers. They represent transition. They are human beings who are walking through the passageway or corridor from youth to adulthood. This passageway is sometimes very dark. It's dark because depending on how much information and guidance sunk into their heart on one side, depends on what comes out on the other side. Yet, until they walk through that corridor, you really never know what you are going to get on the other side. Experiencing a teenager is like walking through a dark tunnel. They are unpredictable and you never know what to expect.

There are developmental differences between the young, old, and teenagers. The same is true with life experiences. All three groups of people go through emotional, psychological and physiological changes that have a tremendous impact on them. Sometimes it appears that teenagers go through the greatest amount of change at one time, placing them in a very delicate position in terms of life. It is like a "crossing over," or rites of passage. No matter how delicate one is over the other, all age groups are equally important in the human experience and life's development. They represent life cycles in this often perplexing journey.

Therefore, as you look at people during different phases of their lives, study them carefully. Whenever you witness a person being born in the world remember the words of Vickie Winans, "The sky shall unfold, preparing His entrance; the stars shall applaud Him with thunders of praise. The sweet light in His eyes shall enhance those awaiting, and we shall behold Him, face-to-face." People are our greatest resource.

Love Versus Respect

Do you know the difference between love and respect? To have respect for a person is to esteem them and to hold a sense of worth or excellence of that individual, their personal qualities and/or their abilities. To respect another is to show honor, regard, and consideration for them.

When one is honored, they are treated with honesty, fairness and integrity in word and deed. So when a person truly honors someone else, they highly respect them. They value them and deem them highly worthy individuals with merit and will place them in a high ranking position in their life. In essence, that person who is honored and respected will have favor and will be given privileges of association. Their requests are usually acted upon by the one who honors and respect them.

To show regard and consideration for someone is to look upon them or think of them with a particular feeling and to take them into account. When you show regard for an individual, you take care of them, pay attention to them, and carefully observe them. Taking someone into consideration causes you to keep that person in mind as important and consequential. You will also tend to factor them in when forming a judgment or making a decision.

Love is the ultimate law of the universe and is the creative force of which everything exists. Love encompasses respect; and is much greater than respect. Therefore, one who loves can learn to respect. Yet it is much more difficult to learn to respect that which you do not love.

The Marriage Bed

Marriage is a wonderful experience and path to walk. Sharing your life with someone else within the context of the ultimate committed relationship is a serious step and designed to last a lifetime. Sometimes it does not always happen that way for a variety of reasons, yet if enough people work at it, respect and honor its condition, set aside the jokes poking fun at and opposing the principles necessary to make it work, perhaps, it might be a happier experience.

In marriage there are many lessons to be learned. No matter how many times you have tried to walk this walk and gave up, the experience gained is profound and will help anyone grow in the most amazing ways. Many lessons come over time and as a result of struggling through the process. Therefore, it is important to stay the course. Both men and women become teachers and students of each other. They must be willing to counsel one another, as well as learn from each other. The tongue becomes one of the most vital tools or deadliest weapons and must be used wisely. The One is the ever present guide and when both husband and wife open up to allow the other in completely, The One inspires love and harmony on many levels and a trust so divine.

There are very distinct roles between men and women. These roles become very apparent in marriage, yet sometimes misunderstood. Men and women have different make-ups and when two people live together, they become like sand paper to one another helping the other to smooth out the rough parts. Sometimes this can feel like hell. When you combine that with the general looseness of how people respond to marriage and the marriage relationship, it can compel one to believe that it is not all that it is cut out to be, when in fact, it is that and then some.

Men and women have different strengths and weaknesses. The weaknesses of one are often compensated for in a marriage relationship by the other partner. When the two learn to co-exist and work effectively together the way The One designed, each can counterbalance their mate's weaknesses. When husbands and wives work together as a cohesive unit or "one flesh," they can move mountains; and in marriage many mountains do come.

How two people are able to handle situations and overcome challenges together is a lesson that we have to learn in any relationship dynamic. Yet, to create a relationship that is exclusive to only the two in the relationship can be very difficult for others to accept, appreciate, or cope with. Sometimes the couple themselves experience difficulty in keeping their relationship closed.

Men are natural-born leaders. This does not negate a woman's ability to lead. We are very capable of leading and have demonstrated that time and time again. However, men are natural leaders and are equipped from birth to lead. Does this mean that a woman will not take the lead on certain things in the marriage? No! It means that generally speaking, men are logical thinkers and able to govern under various situations and circumstances without being directly effected as deeply from environ-mental or outside factors as women are. Women are more effective leaders outside of the home where there is less emotional attachment to the leadership dynamic. Men are more effective leaders when they have the support of a woman in their life. They develop a stronger desire to lead when there is a woman working with them.

In the marriage scenario, both are equally important. Women naturally look for strong leadership in men because this is the vulnerable aspect of who she is. Many women effectively serve as the head and premier leader in their home, yet we are more impactful and fulfilled when we are serving in a co-leadership or supporting leadership role within the home.

Men are the natural head of the home, while women are the neck. Therefore, a head is unable to sit strong and tall without the support of the neck. It is not able to move freely and with direction without a neck. Likewise, a neck has no real purpose or reason without the head because it was designed to support the head. If there were no head, what is the purpose for the neck? The head tells the neck where it wants to move, and then the neck moves it in that direction. Be clear, every human being was born with a purpose and a reason. Yet, if man did not exist, what would be the reason for woman? Woman was created to help man.

A man fit for marriage is a good husbandman. He leads his home fully aware that he too is directed by an unseen force - The One. He exercises his leadership with justice, by being an example of a good steward and lives a life of integrity. He is equitable and straightforward in all of his dealings. He is neither crooked nor despised. He is not impaired with false pride and sneakiness. A good husbandman recognizes that there is a power greater than himself who grants him power and leads him to success. He is aware of his need for his wife and that his favor and success lies in his treatment of her. Therefore, he yields to her full access to his affairs and does not take her power lightly. He knows that generosity to her is generosity to himself, because they are one.

A good husband is humble and is mastering the art of listening. He employs wisdom in dealing with women, placing his wife above them all. He plants like the wise farmer, sowing seeds of life that may yield abundantly. He tills the land of her fertile heart and mind, so that she may take care of him and multiply that which she receives. A good husband is mindful and pays attention to his wife and is aware of the trappings of the foolish and wicked so that he does not get tripped up. He understands that "a man who findeth a wife finds a good thing," and thus is kind to her holding no animosity or contempt for her in his heart. He knows the significance of his wife in his life and therefore dreads going out without his cover and balance.

A good husbandman is astute and has a discerning spirit. He avoids the trappings of, cunningly abhorrent beings seeking to drive a wedge and sow seeds of dissension between him and his wife. He is firm in rejecting the subtle innuendos of other women seeking to lure and charm him into binding ties with them. He trusts in his wife's intuition and counsels with her often regarding such affairs.

A woman fit for marriage is a help-meet, supports her husband, and relieves his burden. She manages her tongue to speak life in all situations. She lifts her husband up and protects his good name. She favors him in public and private, while protecting his reputation. She exalts her husband and quiets her tongue when necessary and diligently works to help him build. A good wife keeps oil in her lamp and a supply on hand, so that there can always be a fire burning. She is prudent in the business of her household, and subtle in other affairs that she may maintain her delicacy. She hides her power when it is expedient to do so and her products are edifying.

A good wife is gentle and kind to her husband without despising him. She trusts his judgment and knows that she is in his head and heart. She uses her intuitive gifts for good and recognizes the voice of The One even through her husband. She takes heed to the voice of truth and naturally prepares herself consistently to become better. A good wife is not afraid to be who she is in The One. She follows not the discourse of those who slander and gossip, or the way of the busybody.

She does not waste her time in idle and vain talk. She is not like the foolish virgin who failed to get oil for her lamp. A good wife envelops her husband and does not let the temptress catch him alone, whispering in his ear as to cause him to become disoriented and lose his way. A good wife has a strong husband, yet even still, she understands the need to be careful and to guard her home planting hedges of protection around it at every turn. She does not stir her husband's wrath provoking him to become insolent, where he is smitten with provocation.

A good wife is keenly refined and genteel and grants that to her own husband to bewilder and vanquish any conniving and wily one coveting what she has. She remembers the unseen power that moves every mountain, even as small as a little annoyance. Her creativity overflows, her light shines, and she recognizes that it is her connection to the Divine that gives her, her radiance.

Husbandman and Helpmeet are friends to each other. They love one another, even as they are loved. They are an example of decency and moral conviction and allow nothing and no one to cause a breach between them. They are constant and sincere in exerting toward one another and relinquishing all others. Pure love drives them to forsake all others, keeping the Creator first.

The two of them in harmony commit their concerns and hardships to The Most High. They understand their longevity and success depends on their ability to release and unbound times of yore. They know that the bondage of their pasts will not serve them well hereafter because it is tainted. They work together and are mindful of The

One, one another, and their obligations. They walk a straight path so as to remove all blemishes and obstacles.

Husband and wife have a propensity to their charge and fortress. As long as they incline to one another in all liveliness, they shall always remain fixed and shall not thirst, nor hunger to be satisfied elsewhere. They keep their confidences among themselves and any uncertainties shall be resolved through mutual consent. They are companions on a journey to a higher plane of existence.

Husbandman and helpmeet learns the necessity of atoning, living life, loving purely, laughing hysterically, and receiving joy. The two gathers together in harmony inviting The One into a three-cord bond that serves as a lifeline for all others that are called within their sphere of influence. Husband and wife understand that they are a gift to each other and are joined in – Holy Matrimony!

Ties That Bind

Love is the most powerful force in the universe. There are many aspects and dimensions of love, yet when the Creator is at the center, we are blessed with true love, which is lasting, satisfying and gratifying. Pure, unconditional love is planted into the heart by the Infinite Heart and Mind, then watered and nourished in such a way that those who carry the seed and those who are reapers of the harvest of it are blessed beyond measure.

The special bond between husband and wife is likened to the love that each one has for the Creator. It is through the expression of love between a man and his help-meet that reveals what each think and feel about God.

Throughout the many books of scripture, reference is made to the unique and divine relationship of married couples. They teach us that husband and wife shall tend to the things that please one another and lift each other up as the Lord tended to the things of the church.

Marriage is not a lightweight affair. It is a condition that requires total commitment and unconditional love in order to stand the test of time. While struggle may be a natural part of life, we have the wonderful opportunity to decide who we choose to struggle with. Until there is a full and complete commitment, a three-cord divine unbreakable bond will not be established – making the ties of marriage weak and painful. A full and complete commitment opens the gateway for a couple to experience marriage in the way that The One intended.

Love is wonderful and new. Love is beautiful. Love is God. God is all things. While in love, you may experience un-pleasantries. Despair not; if you remain faithful they will fade away. Love gives you the faith that "this too shall pass." Spark romance in your life and relationship. Be creative in expressing your love to your covenant partner. The years should never be a reason or excuse to let romance die. Do not become so familiar with each other as to not keep the fire burning. Let there be continuous growth. Keep passion alive, maintaining a high level of energy, willingness, and commitment to the process and journey. Slow down and enjoy the ride.

The Voice of Truth

Transformation is about embarking upon a life-changing journey that inspires you to become your ultimate best. Regardless of the struggles you have in your life or the challenges you may be facing at this moment, you can overcome them with focus and intention. There is a power innate within your being, and it's up to you to take the necessary time to discover the beauty that is within and manifest that person to the world. Discover your purpose in life. Unfold the amazing truth about yourself.

Whenever you are confronted with a problem, take it to the altar of your faith. Leave it there and walk away knowing that it is dealt with. The internal force within is far greater than any problem you may face externally. Believe it. Be aware that you are constantly being guided. Sometimes in this chaotic world there may be confusion; and it can be difficult to hear the voice of truth from within. Tune in and listen carefully to that beacon of light. Therein is real peace and solace.

When you engage in conversation with your inner being it opens the way for deeper understanding of your soul's heartbeat. There is no shame in questioning the ever-present being about the reality of whom you are and the truth in which you were created. Sometimes people take for granted the little things that does not require much thought. The key is to think about those little nuances that sets you apart from others. There is a message to be understood.

Create a team among the three dimensions of your being: body, mind, and spirit. Call the three into harmony as to create a one flesh union. Let them walk in agreement. There are many members of your being, but they are all a part of one body. Let them be in alignment for the good of the whole - body that is. Work to establish optimum balance between all areas of your being that will transcend and move beyond just physical manifestation.

Let the essence of your being experience the depth while you move and flow completely in the spirit. Mine out the precious gifts that you have within. Let your heart touch the heart of others, by allowing the voice of truth to resonate in your walk. Let your walk be one of substance, character, principles, and integrity. More importantly, have heart, and make heart-to-heart connections that quicken others to live and move more freely and completely.

After all, the ultimate law of the universe is love; and if you are not loving, then you are not living- for to love is to live. Your success is attributed to love for self, love for The One and love for humanity. Keep in mind though that success is not necessarily about material gains. Success is about walking in your purpose and also being able to reap the rewards, which includes material necessities and comforts.

Like every snowflake that falls and every finger print, you are unique in the fact that you are who you are and were born to be. There is, has never been, nor will there ever be anyone in the world like you. While you may have similarities to others who have walked the path, the familiarity is only the divine energy or indwelling spirit within that person. You are uniquely you.

So when you look at your fellow man, look as if you are looking at the face of The One and a manifestation of God in flesh. Represent a characteristic of The One well. Remember that you are vastly different, yet are an important piece of the puzzle, designed to fit nicely in the larger scheme of things. Therefore, strike a balance in your reasoning. Challenge yourself to be bold and courageous in being a voice of truth and be willing to stand in in that truth without shame or guilt.

Listen to that quiet still voice within that is there guiding you. It happens to all of us. However, some people keep that message to themselves or hidden deep within. Do not be afraid to share it with the world. Be a transmitter of light and loving energy to help others elevate their vibrations. Be a conduit to enlightenment. Give yourself permission to achieve harmony and balance in your life. Be a resounding vessel to help humanity become whole.

Intuition is a right brain process that allows a person to tap into their subconscious mind to receive and provide guidance. Intuition is discernment, a fact or truth that is independent of any sort of reasoning; but rather on an inner-knowing. Let your inner-knowing be the voice of truth to guide you on your journey. Allow meditation to be a catalyst for reflection and contemplation. Get quiet to hear the Divine talking. Meditation is when you listen and The One talks. How can you learn and be guided when there's constant chattering in your head? Embrace the peace that meditation offers, and remove yourself from the noise and chatter. It's necessary for internal peace. Let your greatest strength be in the power of love. Be willing to walk the walk practicing transparency. Be willing to do the work. Be willing to become one with the voice of truth.

The Miracle of Love

Fellow ones on the path to enlightenment, I thought about you today and wanted you to know that you are truly appreciated and loved. While my words in no way stands alone, I do however come in the spirit of the infinite mind of wisdom, peace, love, compassion, and truth. Bearing witness to The One who stands alone and has power over all things, yet yields some of that authority to those traveling in search of self.

Regardless as to the weight my words carry or the impact they have in your day or even your life at this moment, I personally wanted and felt the need to take time out of my "busy day" to thank you for everything that you are. Sometimes as we get "bogged down" with the issues and challenges of life, it doesn't always appear that a person is as sensitive or as aware as others might think or feel they should be. Please know beloved that my heart beats for you to receive the most beautiful blessing from on high. I send positive energy your way as you journey.

The path of enlightenment encourages subdued strength, mindful awareness, and keen sensitivity. As I reflect on this moment, this space and this time, peace and contentment of mind is a precious gift to behold and I wish it for you and your family. Let your yearning be for wisdom and a heart filled with universal love transcending all that divides. The miracle of love allows us to know that regardless of our station we are continuously being shaped and molded. There is no greater love than one who is willing to dedicate his life to uplift humanity.

On this path we learn many lessons. While I do not have all of the answers or solutions to the challenges that face humanity, there is an intuitive sense that our ultimate success depends on moving synergistically by a spirit generated from universal love and compassion. When one can realize harmony, they can actually "see" God working. As you observe the cohesiveness of the nine systems of our body cooperatively working together or the nine planets as they revolve around the sun, you can witness this harmony at work. The unity within the planetary system keeps all planets in their orbit; and concord within the biological system keeps the body alive.

Every planet in the universe and every organ in the body operate within a divine law and unyieldingly submit and surrender wholly to the Infinite Wisdom that initiates its effective operation. When there is imbalance or disease, the systems' operation ultimately begins to shut down. The absence of love produces imbalance and disease. Love is the creative force of all things in existence. Love, is the miracle that make things do what they do. Unification in the spirit of love conquers all that is in contrary.

When we come together in the Spirit of Love, The One is always present, for God is love. Love is the Creator of life. It sustains life, because it is life. Love brings forth life from every kind and is expressed in many forms. Its attributes are clear and it has a distinctive quality, trait, characteristic, and mannerism. One of the most beautiful gifts from above is the spirit of harmony and agreement. Yet, it is born of love. Love above all else is life-changing and is the greatest miracle. Again, if you have not loved, you have not lived.

Every human being is born into the world through the vicissitudes of the pain and struggle of "labor." Yet the labor was not in vain. As each of us entered this world unknown and very different from that familiar place of comfort we call "womb," it was The One present expressing infinity through mother, father, aunt, uncle, sister, brother, grandmother, grandfather, and cousin. Today, it is The One present who continues to guide us every step of the way on our journey, expressing through friend, son, daughter, stranger, teacher, pastor, doctor, nurse, co-worker, opponent, competitor, and team mate.

There is a saying by Bill Wilson, "to the world you may be one person, but to one person you may be the world." When love touches the heart of another, it is profound because at that moment it is only love existing, yet giving birth to all. I took this time to send loving thoughts your way. No matter which road we take in life, love is the path to enlightenment. The people you touch along the way with the hand of love will always be remembered and the kindness you show will be cherished forever.

May you always remain constant in love, for it truly is the miracle of life.

Change

Change is a natural course of life. It's not unusual to experience a variety of changes throughout life. Why fear it? Great things happen on the verge of change. If you get stuck in a rut or your ways for that matter, the only way to get out of it is to do something different than what you had been doing. If your behavior doesn't change, nor will your condition.

The idea of an alteration from the norm is for things to get better than they already are. Change is meant to help you take a step forward, not backwards. Therefore, there is nothing to be anxious about. A little apprehension about the unknown is natural, but no need to fight the modification of things or the agents of change.

You know, the interesting thing is that the more things change, the more they stay the same. However, you really don't arrive at that point until you are able to actually embrace the changes in your life. Change is really nothing more than innovation. Be that enthusiastic innovator who knows how to bring things and situations to modern times. Break those old habits that don't serve you well. There is no need to be weighed down with stuff you no longer need.

Think about this for a moment. Spring, summer, winter, and fall are seasons; but they are also opportunities for growth and renewal. The various seasons provide a glimpse of how things change. Fall teaches us the importance of shedding the old to allow for the ushering in of the new. Winter teaches us the need to rest, restore, and renew. Spring teaches us that once the proper rest has occurred, we are able to come forth more refreshed, new, and lively. Summer teaches us the concept of climaxing and reaching peaks, while enjoying the harvest of our labor.

Life cycles represent points of change as well. Likewise, there are stages and degrees of change. Look at the life cycle of the human being. One key element in all circumstances of change is that the product which is undergoing a makeover needs to be nurtured through the process of change. Change is the exchange of ideas. Let your change be a conversation with the Originator, who knew what was in mind when you were created.

Don't be afraid to become the idea that was in the mind of the Infinite from the very beginning. That is what change is all about.

The Chicken or the Egg

What say you about the beauty of two becoming one? Life is precious and to ask which got here first the chicken or the egg is like asking which is more important the mother or the child. It really doesn't matter who came first, because life is such that the child becomes the parent, and the parent is the child.

Who is more important? It's simple. Both the chicken and the egg are equally important. Without the seed of life, life could not be. Without a firm resting place, life could not be. Life will not and cannot take place without two becoming one. So you ask about partheno-genesis? What about it? Okay, it is a situation where an egg develops into a new individual without it being fertilized. So tell me. How did the egg get there?

The sperm fertilizes the ovum. Yet, if there was no ovum to fertilize, the sperm would continuously swim to an endless destination with no place to go or no purpose. If the ovum had no sperm to fertilize it, it would dissipate – wither away and die. It is the power of the two becoming one that creates this wonderfully magnificent explosion of life. So you ask again about parthenogenesis? What about it? In parthenogenesis there is still the power of two becoming one. They are either similar or dissimilar. What say ye?

A man without a wife travels consistently in search of that special one to join with. If he does not find her, he continues wandering on with no purpose or direction. A woman without a husband is warm and ready, looking in every direction for whence her savior comes to subdue her. Yet, if he is nowhere in sight, she cools ever so quickly and slowly dries up.

Life is a result of two becoming one. If you must know the answer to the question of who came first – the chicken or the egg? The answer is simple and tis true.

I came first, and then there was U!

The Power and Beauty of the Tongue

The tongue is beautiful yet powerful, small yet big. It is a helpful tool that the Creator gave us to move mountains. It can be used to save lives and slay the enemy of freedom, justice, and equality. It is so light in comparison to the rest of the armor of God, a powerful weapon for good, yet easily concealed - A mighty sword.

It can transform lives, impart truth and wisdom. It provides encouragement upon one's heart in times of need. It can leave a smile upon one's face and serve as a vehicle to pass on vital information and guidance through generations to come. It can be used to slay the enemy of truth, or to destroy falsehood. It can save a life, mend a broken heart, or lift the spirits of another.

The tongue can inspire and provide hope. It's a miracle, and a tool to do angelic works, placing blessings upon one's life. We can use it to bring to fruition our gifts and talents, as well as give life and love. We can bless others through good words and good works. We can use it to realize our dreams and help others to realize theirs. We can use it to provide constructive feedback.

Learning to utilize the tongue to the greater good is truly an art and science. Using it to benefit humanity is a miracle. The tongue is a precious gift from above. It is a symbol of faith. It is the tool used to accept, profess, and reflect the Word. Thank you to the Most High, for such a powerful and beautiful gift...The Power of the tongue moves the world. Let's strive to use it wisely.

Synergize Your Mind

We can discuss the concept of synergizing the mind in order to take control of our destiny. This is a pertinent conversation to have. In raising the level of consciousness with respect to this way of interacting with others, we must first understand what the terms synergy and synergize means.

Synergy is the combined action that allows anything to be accomplished. To synergize is to increase one's effectiveness by bringing together all components cooperatively. In this case, we are synergizing the mind. In order to synergize the mind –mind, body, and spirit must be working together in harmony for us to achieve our greatest potential. Synergy is the foundation and spring-board for group empowerment.

The intention behind your actions, will determine your outcome. By evaluating and analyzing the intentions and motives behind what you do, you can better accept the truth of your expectations. Expectations are directly linked to whether or not you become satisfied. Likewise, achieving satisfaction helps you to perform optimally. It is a fact that people perform better when they enjoy what they do. Even when positivity and creativity overflow, our interactions with others are simply more fulfilling when our expectations are met. When we perform well, we communicate more effectively; and effective communication is critically important when building teams.

Everyone on your team or in your circle must be on the same page or of like minds. The integrity of your team depends on its collective cooperation and participation, and the soundness of its members. Every team member comes to the table with individual ideas or concepts. However, strong teams are built on strategic mergence. Strategic mergence is focused energy exerted for the intended purpose of unification into a single body or cell – Synergy!

In order for there to be a merging, there must be a "master mind." This master mind is the overall mission of the group. This shared goal becomes the universal thought, idea, and concept, which allows the collective thoughts and mindset of the many to become aligned and manifest as one single objective. Strong teams are interdependent; and each team member is able to take ownership of the idea or mission. Do you understand why? It is because, it is their idea.

To synergize your mind is to increase your effectiveness by unifying the conscious, subconscious, and super-conscious departments of your mind. The conscious mind is referred to as the human mind and sees things as they appear to be; it sees limitations and impossibilities, yet makes impressions in the subconscious. The subconscious mind is like the rudder of a ship being guided by the captain. It is like a steering wheel of a car that is being directed by a driver. The subconscious mind captures every detail of what we feel deeply or imagine clearly. The super-conscious mind is our "creative" mind. It recognizes our true purpose and flashes "perfect ideas" across our conscious mind.

By recognizing the unique connection between the three, we are better able to use our conscious mind to make positive suggestions to our subconscious. As we consistently shape our conscious mind to think harmoniously, peacefully, constructively, creatively, and in-purpose, we enable our subconscious to create those circumstances and conditions. Our super-conscious mind then confirms them and attaches our ideas to a higher purpose, opening up the universe for us to experience that which we sincerely desire. All of this is done by the power of synergy.

Objective Reality

Success does not happen by chance. We create it by visualizing in our mind's eye the possibilities of what could be. After that, we must focus our energy in the direction of that which we see, then back it by motion. Everything of value has a price attached to it. However, the cost is not necessarily a monetary one. When we seek to attain something of value, it requires us to exert energy and carve out time, otherwise we fall short in achieving it. When we aim for something, we generate ideas and project those thoughts into the atmosphere. At the moment of projection, we are actually engaging in the "act of visualizing an idea as an objective reality."

An objective reality is truth manifested in the tangible or physical realm. When we actively participate in this process, we are able to catch a glimpse of the endless possibilities. However, we must apply ourselves in order to bring the conceptualization into existence. Transformation begins in the mind! Whatever we are able to see in our mind's eye, we have the power to bring into fruition. This is an innate ability of all human beings.

Free Your Mind

Have you not heard the story of the flea and the elephant? It provides a powerful illustration of how one can be placed in mental bondage through the power of suggestion. Your world can be colored and out of that coloring your reality affected.

A flea can usually under normal conditions jump about eighteen inches high. However, if you put a flea in a jar and close the lid, an interesting thing happens. You see, the flea initially will jump the height of what they have the ability to jump. However, with each jump comes the realization that there is a blockage creating an impediment of normal and natural height. In this case, the lid is hindering the flea from going as high as it could naturally.

Over time, the flea will believe that it can only jump the height of the jar as a result of the lid. Of course, this is not true, but the flea was led to believe that through a conditioning process. So when the lid is removed, the flea will still continue to jump the height of the jar; and although its natural ability is to be able to jump eighteen inches, it will continue to perform at a much lower level than its ability although the lid has been removed.

The same is true with an elephant that has been chained down for several years with a big ball and chain. Although the ball and chains have been replaced with a thin rope, the elephant will not break free because it does not know its own strength and ability. Therefore, the elephant as big and powerful as it is will remained tied up.

In order to stop the perpetuation of negative thinking and the conditioning of your mind, you must become the producer of your own thoughts. Be the creator of your reality and understand that the possibilities are limitless. When we produce thoughts, we are actually involved in the process of thinking and generating original ideas –thus being mentally active. When a person is mentally active, he or she is in a state of being energetic and lively as it pertains to the mind. They are using force and energy, while being engaged in perpetual motion.

A mentally active person possesses enthusiasm. The state of mental activity is a prerequisite to being physically active. Everything you see is a physical manifestation of a mental reality. How mentally active are you? Are you like the flea or the elephant, unable to operate at full potential because someone has suggested to you that you are not capable? Are you still in bondage from an impediment from your past and have failed to realize that your condition has changed? Do you not understand that you are free, and therefore it is time to free your mind?

Imagine Yourself

Without an image in your mind, there is nothing to move toward. Everything we see externally begins with a thought in the mind. It is a visualization of yours or someone else's. Thoughts create motion, which produces a physical reality. The more we generate positive thoughts, the more favorable our reality becomes. Elevated thinking transforms life. Have you heard the phrase, "if you keep doing what you're doing, you will keep getting what you've got?" The point is if nothing changes, nothing changes.

Be enthusiastic. Act within the framework of your ability to bring things into existence that does not already exist physically. No need to battle, just do it through the Law of Non-resistance. Nothing is able to resist a person who is completely non-resistant. When we resist something, we give it power by acknowledging its presence, and spend unnecessary energy that could better be spent on other endeavors.

Look at water for a moment. Have you noticed how it keeps going regardless as to what obstacle is presented? It is so non-resistant that even a rock placed in its path, does not stop its flow. If the rock stays in the path, the water will eventually wear away the rock. There is a lesson in this for the astute and attentive mind.

You have extraordinary power over your own circumstances. Know thyself. Go within the depths of your being and discover the fascinating and glorious you. Imagine yourself, and then Be! It is so.

About the Author

 Atiya, founder of The Marriage Tree, has over the past 20 years, dedicated her life to honing her craft and, indeed, her calling – to empower, build and maximize hu-potential by affecting profound transformation in people's attitudes, perspectives and behaviors. She has been the catalyst responsible for inspiring countless people worldwide to realize their dreams and achieve joy, success and fulfill-ment in life.

Now she's bringing all her past experiences, education, and business-development skills from her considerable history as a speaker, author and life coach to focus on her core message: marital harmony ~ extended and profound.

Yes! It is possible to have an enduring relation-ship that is a positive and rewarding experience for both partners. But like anything of value, it requires fine-tuning and the willingness to learn to navigate the intricacies and subtleties of the changes any marriage encounters during its lifetime. Marriage is organic – it changes, evolves, grows - or like many living things, without proper nurturing, it can deteriorate. But the good news is: it doesn't have to break down. Building a history is a worthwhile, satisfying goal, as well as a tangible legacy for your children.

Atiya is at once an optimist and a pragmatist. She's a firm believer in the reality of a happy and satisfying long term marriage. But she's no Pollyanna, having herself encountered the vagaries of marriages over the past 21 years. She has come through them stronger and happier, gratefully committed, and she can help you to achieve the same result! She'll be the first to tell that what she's going to show you won't be easy, but she's sure of one thing – it will be worth it!

You deserve to live a life filled with mutual inspiration and genuine respect. Atiya has the resources – intellectually and empathetically - to guide you to fruitful solutions that will not only positively-impact your relationship, but, as importantly, will leave you personally empowered.

Other Books by Atiya

From Ordinary to Extraordinary

Purposeful Dating

Hidden Pearls

The Beauty of Being Free

Audios by Atiya

Petals of a Rose audiobook

Love is Not a Game

Overcoming the Pain of Losing a Mother

This is Atiya

Taking Back Your Life and Power